KU-566-000

DISCARDED
Libraries

60000510032

THIS BOOK BELONGS TO

....

WEST NORTHAMPTONSHIRE COUNCIL	
60000510032	
Askews & Holts	
CC	

HarperCollins*Publishers*
1st Floor, Watermarque Building, Ringsend Road
Dublin 4, Ireland

Text copyright © Farshore 2022
Interior illustration copyright © Dynamo 2022
The moral rights of the author and illustrator have been asserted.

Special thanks to Rachel Delahaye
With thanks to Speckled Pen for their help in the development of this series.

ISBN 978 0 00 851248 4
Printed and bound in the UK using 100% renewable electricity at CPI Group (UK) Ltd
1

A CIP catalogue record for this title is available from the British Library.

All rights reserved. No part of this publication may be reproduced,
stored in a retrieval system, or transmitted, in any form or by any means,
electronic, mechanical, photocopying, recording or otherwise, without
the prior permission of the publisher and copyright owner.

Stay safe online. Any website addresses listed in this book are correct at the time
of going to print. However, Farshore is not responsible for content hosted by
third parties. Please be aware that online content can be subject to change
and websites can contain content that is unsuitable for children.
We advise that all children are supervised when using the internet.

MIX
Paper from
responsible sources
FSC™ C007454

This book is produced from independently certified FSC™ paper
to ensure responsible forest management.

For more information visit: www.harpercollins.co.uk/green

SUPER CUTE

THE SEASIDE
RESCUE

PIP BIRD

Farshore

CONTENTS

CHAPTER ONE: **Breezing Along**   1

CHAPTER TWO: **Off to the Beach We Go!**   21

CHAPTER THREE: **Sandy Days and Spooky Frights**   40

CHAPTER FOUR: **The Tale of the Wail**   55

CHAPTER FIVE: **Rise and Shine!**   71

CHAPTER SIX: **Follow the Hugs**   85

CHAPTER SEVEN: **Treasure Beyond Measure**   101

CHAPTER EIGHT: **Good Bye, Good Rock**   115

CHAPTER ONE

Breezing Along

'WEE! WEE! WEEEEEE! Look at me, so wild and free!'

The super cutes looked up at their friend, Pip the pineapple, who was very high in the air. How she'd got there, they didn't know – but there she was, way up above the treetops, tumbling like a fruit-shaped circus performer.

Pip was loving every minute. She had never

done such incredible acrobatics. As she somersaulted over and over, she had a revolving view of her home, the wonderful World of Cute. When she was facing up, she could see its wide blue sky, filled with popsicle parrots and flying sweetie pies. When she was facing down, she saw the dipsy daisy fields blooming beneath her. And when she was the right way round, she could

see all of Charm Glade. The pretty town was filled with cutes, going about their business, buying fruit sodas, exchanging books and making crafts in their front gardens. Everything looked cute-iful. And something smelled good, too . . .

Pip turned her head and saw – sugar puffs! Giant clouds of sweet sticky dust coming from the direction of the marshmallow factory at the edge of town!

'This is amazing!' she cried down to her friends. 'And delicious!'

'Pip! Please concentrate,' Cami cried.

'Be careful!' Louis barked.

Pip wasn't listening. She just grinned and waved. Cami the cloud was her oldest friend, along with Sammy the sloth. She'd met Lucky the lunacorn and Dee the dumpling kitty at the talent show, and then Louis the labradoodle and Micky the mini-pig at a sleepover party in the museum. Now they were all inseparable.

The super cutes been playing in the meadow when Pip had run ahead to get in some cartwheels and backflips. But while attempting a triple-whipple-flip, she'd got caught up in a thermal ripple. The raspberry-flavoured gust of wind spiralled up and up and up into the sky, taking the pineapple with it.

Pip wasn't afraid of heights. Up here, she could do the most incredible gymnastics, like an extra swooshy double-swirl and maybe she should try a TRIPLE-swirl –

Louis barked louder, waking her from her sporty trance. Pip suddenly realised something. The thermal ripple had reached its limit and was now on its way back down – FAST. And there was nothing between her and the ground, way below. Uh oh!

'Oh dear!' cried Pip. 'Help!'

Lucky flew up into the air beside the

frightened pineapple. 'Pip, you'll be fine,' she said calmly. 'I'll fly underneath you and catch you on my back. Just try not to prickle me!'

The lunacorn swooped beneath the tumbling fruit cute and caught her perfectly. There was a small prickle moment as Pip landed upside down on Lucky's back, but she was safe and

that was the most important thing. When they reached the ground, everyone cheered.

'You were lucky, Pip,' Sammy said. 'On windy days like these, thermal ripples can go crazy. And I think the wind is picking up.' The sloth's fur changed colour depending on where he was and how he was feeling. Right now, it was brown and waving in the breeze, which was definitely getting stronger.

'I didn't mean to catch a ripple,' Pip panted. 'But it was lots of fun. There were sugar puffs and the air was so fresh and free!'

'Sugar puffs . . . from the marshmallow factory?' Sammy said, full of concern. 'Oh my! The wind really is strong if they've blown all the way to Charm Glade. Doesn't happen very often.'

'Then let's make the most of it and catch another ripple!' Pip urged. 'Not just me – all of us! And we'll be careful. Cami can let us know when it getting too windy, can't you, Cami?'

The little cloud didn't look sure. The wind was already whipping her into a candyfloss cone!

'I've got an idea,' said Dee the Dumpling Kitty, pulling out threads and knitting needles from her bottomless craft pockets. 'I'll make a kite carpet that we can all fly on.'

'In all my days working at the Museum of the Magic and Marvellous, I've never ever heard of a kite carpet,' said Micky the mini-pig.

'I think that might be because she's only just

invented it,' said Sammy.

'Correct!' said the crafty kitten. She was knitting so quickly, the kitty knitting was a blur.

'If you've only just thought of it, then how do you know if it works?' Micky quizzed.

'We don't until we try it out! Ta-da!' Dee smiled triumphantly and revealed a beautiful carpet, woven with multi-coloured threads and ribbons. It was big enough for everyone!

'Let's try it now. Over there!' Pip cried, pointing to an area of the meadow where the Dipsy Daisies were giggling. 'I think the Dipsy Daisies are being tickled by a rising ripple. Any second now it'll go up and up. Let's catch it! Come on, super cutes!'

The friends placed their kite carpet next to the giggling flowers and jumped on just in time – WHOOSH! – before they were lifted on the spiralling, fruity breeze.

'This is incredible!' Micky said, peering over

the edge.

'And so pretty,' said Cami, pointing to the carpet's ribbons, which fluttered behind them like streamers.

'And perfectly safe, see?' Pip somersaulted across the carpet to Micky.

Cami wobbled a little. 'Um, everyone?' she said. 'I think there's a really big wind on the way.'

'Don't worry, we'll be safe on the carpet,' said Dee. 'We can use the ribbons as seat-belts, and I've sewn pockets underneath. The wind will fill the pockets and turn them into air pillows. Perfect for a soft landing.'

'One problem,' shouted Sammy over the roar of the incoming wind. 'What if we don't land at all?'

The super cutes looked down. They weren't hovering above the Dipsy Daisy Field any more, but speeding over Charm Glade on the fast-moving windy current.

'Where are we going?' Cami said nervously.

'Who knows? It's an adventure!' cried Pip.

The kite carpet whizzed through the sky. Below them, the World of Cute was like a carnival. Cutes on the ground were making the most of the windy weather, flying kites of all colours which looped and danced on the wind. Flags fluttered and the leaves from the maple syrup trees skittered through the streets. Sweetie Pies and Cackle Birds swooped for fun on the raspberry thermal ripples, and the wind piped sweet tunes through the Tootle-Fruit Flowers.

The super cutes breezed onwards until the wind finally blew itself out. Then the kite carpet

rocked gently like a falling feather, down on to the shores of Sweet Cove.

The smooth, silky sands of the cove could hardly be seen. Instead, the beach was covered with piles and piles of debris. There were broken boats, stranded flamingo floats, upturned pedalos . . . junk strewn from one end to the other.

'There must have a been a big storm out at sea,' Micky said, looking around at the chaos.

'Last time there was a scene like this was

during Cyclone Chaos,' Sammy said.

'I remember that,' said Cami, a little shakily. 'I was blown miles out to sea, then blown back again . . . inside out!'

'Ouch,' Dee said sympathetically. 'And ouch again!'

She pointed to a turtle, lying on its back, legs frantically waving in the air. The gang heaved the turtle over so it was upright, although the poor thing was so shaken it couldn't speak.

'Over here, everyone!' Micky cried.

The super cutes rushed over to see a pile of Jelly Babies, wet and sticky and covered in grains of sand. On their arms were little arm bands. It looked like they'd been having a swimming lesson when the storm hit.

'Poor things,' Pip said. 'That sand must be itchy!'

'I know how that feels,' Sammy said, scratching his bottom in sympathy.

'Where are the clean-up crabs?' Louis asked. 'They're usually in charge of the beaches.'

'Is that them?' Pip said, peering at a row of little legs sticking out of the sand. She dug one out. The crab's stalky eyes waved in alarm and confusion.

'What's going on, Crabby?' asked Lucky.

The clean-up crab dusted down its apron and clacked its pincers. 'Too much, too soon. Don't know where to begin. What a mess. What a mess!' it shrieked and then dived head-first back into the sand.

'We can't leave the clean-up crabs to tidy the whole beach,' Pip said. 'It's a really big job, and they're only small. It will take them forever! They need help.'

'I agree,' said Lucky. 'But I don't know where to start either. It's a total mess!'

'I have just the thing to motivate us,' Micky announced. 'If we make this an organised

event, then it immediately goes into the Hall of
Cute Cooperation at the museum.'

'With teamwork you can achieve anything,'
Louis barked.

'Teamwork makes the dream work,' Pip
cheered.

'How about giving this clean-up a name?'
Lucky said.

'Big Beach Clean?' Dee pondered. 'No . . . not
cute enough.'

'How about Operation Sweet Beach?'
Cami suggested.

'Operation Sweet Beach is perfect!' Pip said,
flipping with glee.

Lucky caught Pip before she landed upside

down on a stranded Paddle Squid. The Paddle Squid was very big. It took the whole gang to help it back into the water, where it blew bubbles and made heart signs with its legs before paddling away. Their first rescue! The cutes cheered as they watched it go.

Someone else was watching, too.

Someone whose whiskers twitched and whose brain whirred with excitement.

A fun day at the beach, rewarded with a mention in the Museum's Hall of Cute Cooperation?

Clive the chihuahua sucked in his cheeks, fluttered his eyelashes and struck a pose.

'Operation Me Me Me, here I come!' he yipped.

CHAPTER TWO

Off to the
Beach We Go!

The super cutes rushed home to get everything
they needed for Operation Sweet Beach. They
met up again under the Wishing Tree, wearing
sensible work dungarees.

'I brought some net bags to collect rubbish,'
said Lucky.

'Excellent,' Sammy said. 'Rubbish always causes problems. We don't want hug whales inhaling glitter balls, or hermit crabs adopting fizzy-pop cans for a shell. I brought along a book which will tells us exactly where all the animals live, to help us return lost nature to its natural habitat.'

'I've brought some gloves to protect us from nasty splinters,' Cami said. 'And I'm full of rain and ready to wash off sandy creatures.'

'I've got a camera to take some photographs for the Hall of Cute Cooperation. And a spade for digging out buried things,' Micky said.

'I've just got my paws for digging,' Louis said. 'But I've made some leaflets to hand out, inviting people to join Operation Sweet Beach,' he added, twitching his pencil nose. Then he sneezed, added a dusting of glitter as a final touch.

'I've brought my swimming costume,' Pip declared. 'We may as well have some fun while we're there.'

'Pip!' Dee purred in amusement. 'Trust you to be sporty even when there's work to do.'

'I can be worky and sporty!' Pip said with a wink. 'I'll swim out and get things that are floating in the water.'

'That way you can keep cool,' Cami added. 'We know how you hate getting too hot.'

Dee patted her backpack. 'And I've got

never-ending
velvet cake and a
bottomless bottle
of cherry lemonade,'
she said.

Lucky licked her lips. 'Today is going to be amazing,' she sighed. 'Helping, playing and then scoffing down delicious things!'

'Hooray!' shouted everyone.

Cami shivered with happiness and started raining down inflatable buckets and spades, which popped with a splashing sound. Pip couldn't contain her excitement. She ran round in circles, tripped over and started to roll away.

'What are we waiting for!' she hollered. 'Let's go!'

They ran all the way to the coast, telling every cute they met about Operation Sweet Beach and handing out Louis' leaflets. Soon there was long conga line of helpers, skipping and singing:

We're off to clean the Sweet Cove sands

Come and join us, holding hands.

We'll tidy up our pretty beach

And life, my friends, will be a peach!

Cooperation! Sweep the beach!

Cooperation! Clean the beach!

Join Operation Sweetest Beach . . .

Here we come!

With so many helpers, putting the beach back in order would take no time at all! But before they even got close to the sea, the cutes had an inkling that something was wrong. There was an extremely loud yapping coming from Sweet Cove. It was as if the angry bark of a very small dog was blasting through huge speakers.

Cami's cloud fluff turned grey. 'Oh dear,' she said, floating up and looking ahead. 'It looks as if we've got company.'

'The more, the better!' said Lucky. 'There's a lot to do!'

Cami frowned. 'Not the helpful sort of company, I'm afraid.'

The cutes arrived at Sweet Cove – and stared in

horror at the little dog in the turquoise sequined bathing costume, lying on a sun-lounger on top of the kite carpet like a glamorous mer-pup. He wore a wide-brimmed hat and sunglasses, with a smoothie in one hand and megaphone in the other.

'CLIVE!' the cutes groaned.

Whenever Clive the chihuahua showed up, there was always drama. Clive loved causing a scene, and he was very, very good at it. From ruining talent shows to stealing prizes, there was nothing he wouldn't do to be the centre of attention. Just when they thought Clive had changed for the better – and the cutes KNEW there was a kind heart underneath the spoilt exterior! – he always did something silly and mean. He demanded new outfits and special food, or announced that he was descended from the most important cute family ever to exist.

'CLEAN UP, CLEAN UP!' Clive yapped through his speaker. 'NO SLACKING. WITH TEAMWORK YOU CAN MAKE THE DREAM WORK!'

'He stole that line from me!' Pip said crossly.

'And if he's so keen on everyone working together, why isn't he joining in?' Sammy sighed. The day had just got a LOT more complicated.

Clive flicked through *Furry and Fabulous* fashion magazine and continued to bark orders. The poor little clean-up crabs scuttled to and fro, snapping their claws and muttering rude things under their breath.

'Forward, not sideways!' Clive yipped. 'Pick it up. Put it over there. Well, move the other thing first . . . I don't know where it goes, just move it!'

'What is he doing?' Micky squeaked in frustration. 'Those poor clean-up crabs are doing their best!'

Pip was so angry, her prickles bristled. 'It's time for a team talk,' she said. 'Gather round and listen up. It's not easy to get rid of Clive

without a big drama, and we don't have time for drama. We need to get the beach cleaned up before nightfall.'

'If we don't finish before the evening tide arrives, all this rubbish will get sucked out to sea,' Sammy added. 'It will be a disaster for all the delicate corals and sea creatures.'

Pip put her hands on her hips. 'Let's ignore Clive and get to work. If he thinks he's in charge, perhaps he'll leave us alone.'

The Operation Sweet Beach crew nodded in agreement. They passed the message down the line to all the cutes that had signed up. Ignore Clive and get on with the job! Then they marched on to the cluttered sands and set about clearing up.

Clive sat upright on his lounger. 'Yoo-hoo, you lot!' he called. 'Welcome to Clive's Glam-Slam Beach Clean. I'll be giving out orders and you follow them, OK?'

The cutes ignored Clive, as agreed. They separated into groups and began to pick through the litter, collecting Cookie Clams and Sand Smiles and other watery creatures that needed to be helped back into the sea.

A low *grrrrrrrrr* rumbled through Clive's megaphone. 'Did you hear me?' he growled.

'We heard you, Clive,' Pip said. 'If you keep giving instructions, we'll keep cleaning.' She looked at Lucky and whispered, 'Well, it's not a lie. We just won't be listening to his instructions!'

'Good, good,' Clive yapped. He adjusted his hat and lowered his glasses. 'Sarah Strawberry, I see you!' he barked. 'What clumsy posture! Back straight, bend at the knees, pluck the litter, stand and dispose. Repeat after me . . . Back straight, bend at the knees . . .'

The strawberry cute tried to ignore him as Pip had suggested, but Clive marched over and placed the megaphone next to her ear. 'Sarah Strawberry, what did I say?' he yelled.

Sarah was so startled that she dropped her bag of litter. The contents spilled back on to the beach.

'Clumsy!' Clive sang, and sashayed back to his lounger. He clicked his fingers and a pizza slice ran to his side, clutching a cool box full of kiwi-granita smoothies.

'What a ridiculous dog,' Sammy muttered.

'The beach is even more of a mess since Clive arrived,' Cami sighed, watching another clean-up crab dive head-first into the sand. 'The poor crabs are sand-diving to get away from him!'

'Let me clear some paths,' Pip said. She powered into a forward roll, catching bits of litter

on her pineapple spikes as she went. 'There! Once you make a start, it isn't so bad. Come on, team. Let's do this!'

'You're MY team,' Clive yelled. 'Don't listen to HER. Listen to ME!'

The cutes looked at each other and rolled their eyes.

'You're very good at team talks,' Micky whispered to Pip.

'Thanks, Micky,' Pip said, doing a happy flip and landing face-down in a huge pile of slippery seaweed. 'Kelp! Kelp!'

Tina the toaster and Vincent the vacuum pulled Pip out and cleaned her up – apart from a sprig of minty moss weed tangled in her spiky top, which Pip kept as a sun hat.

The cutes soon had the beach-cleaning down to an art. Some cutes removed litter and others hunted for stranded animals. When they found an animal, they waved their hands in the air and Cami and Lucky flew in to fix the problem. Cami washed away the sand with her rain, and Lucky flew the animals back to where they came from, with the help of Sammy's information booklet.

Clive didn't lift a finger except to reach for kiwi-granita smoothies. But every now and then, he would sit up and bark through his megaphone.

'Great job, great job!' he shouted. 'I'm really good at this team-leader business. My great

great great uncle Barkly Dewclaw was a colonel, you know. I'm born to lead.'

'Speaking of leads, I wish someone would put one on Clive and take him for walkies miles from here,' Dee hissed.

'Ignore him, Dee,' said Cami.

So that's what they did.

CHAPTER THREE

Sandy Days and Spooky Frights

While Clive lounged about, the real Operation Sweet Beach continued successfully in the background. Bags were filled with junk. Boats were pulled upright. Sand flutes, tambourine stars and sea jellies were taken to Cami's 'cloud wash' before being helped back into the sea.

Clive didn't pick up a single thing. He just pawed through his magazine, and adjusted his position to make his sequined swimming costume the glitteriest it could be. Meanwhile, his friends, the Glamour Gang, made sure he never ran out of fruit salad and ice-cold slushies, and complemented him on his beach fashion.

'With those sparkles, you'll make the mermaids jealous,' said the muffin.

'Your style is simply dazzling,' cooed the pizza slice.

'Best thing on the beach!' the scooter declared.

Usually, words like these were exactly what Clive was after. But the sudden flood of praise seemed to annoy the little chihuahua. He sat upright, whipped off his hat and glasses and pointed to the cutes, who were all busy cleaning.

'THEN WHY AREN'T THEY LOOKING AT ME?' he screamed. 'WHY ARE THEY IGNORING ME?'

'They're c-c-cleaning, just as you told them to,' the snail stammered.

Clive trembled with fury, making his sequins shimmer beautifully. Although nobody dared point that out. 'Yes, but they could at least stop and APPRECIATE me once in a while!' he yipped.

'Help! Help!'

A frightened gherkin was bobbing in the

water just in front of Clive's lounger.

'I'm being pulled out to sea!' the gherkin cried. **'HELP ME!'**

Clive dusted down his ruffled sequins and pretended not to hear.

'Clive!' Lucky shouted. 'Help the gherkin, or he'll get carried off on the tide! Clive!'

But the little dog lifted *Furry and Fabulous* in front of his face and lay back down.

Someone had to help the struggling gherkin! Lucky flapped into the air to get the cutes' attention. Then everyone ran towards the shoreline, with Pip in the lead.

'I don't believe that dog,' Dee miaowed. 'What a selfish little –'

'Wait,' Pip said. She pointed at Clive.

The chihuauhua's wonderful beach hat had blown into the sea, where it was now bobbing upside down on the waves. Clive was looking

at it with desperate, boggly eyes. His chin and
whiskers quivered.

'My hat!' he cried. 'It's a one-of-a-kind design
by Vabarki!'

'Then get it!' shouted Pip.

'You get it,' Clive ordered.

'No, I'm rescuing the gherkin,' said Pip.
'What's the matter, Clive? Don't you want to get
your fur wet?'

Clive was building up to a tantrum – but suddenly stopped. He clawed at the sand, and picked something up. Perhaps he was rescuing a Cookie Clam? It was about time he did something useful!

But no! Clive quickly packed his things in his towel bag and was heading back up the beach, leaving his precious Vabarki designer hat behind.

'Clive, where are you going?' Pip called.

Ignoring Pip, Clive turned to his friends. 'Come on, gang. I'm bored with all this mucking about.'

Clive flounced off towards Charm Glade with his pointy nose high in the air. The Glamour Gang followed. Clive stopped just where the sand met the path, and began to dig.

'What's he up to?' Pip said.

'I can't see from this far away,' Lucky said.

'He's probably just done a poo,' Dee tutted.

'Dogs don't bury their business,' Louis said and then blushed. 'They just leave it.'

'Why do dogs dig holes, then?' Micky said.

'Who knows?' Sammy said. He scratched his bottom in confusion. 'Although I usually do. That's odd.'

'Who cares!' said Pip. 'Let's get on with the job. The sooner it's done, the more time we have for playing. And I can't wait to get stuck into that velvet cake.'

'Mmm, and cherry lemonade,' Cami sighed.

The Operation Sweet Beach task force worked hard. They sang to keep their spirits up and solved problems together. Cami washed creatures with her plentiful, fresh rain. Sammy located habitats and Lucky flew lost creatures home. Louis ran as a messenger between them all. Micky litter-picked with a gang of helpful cutes. Pip swam out to sea and back, again and again, clearing away all the rubbish in the crystal water.

Soon

everything

was spick

and span.

Operation Sweet

Beach had been a huge success!

'Look!' said Cami, pointing back out to sea.

Blushing pinks and juicy oranges filled the

sky, and the sun sat like a warm apricot on the

horizon. 'Isn't it beautiful?'

'Just like our beach,' Lucky said.

'And our world,' Louis barked softly.

'And our friendship and cooperation,' said Pip.

'And it's time for cake,' said Dee. 'Let's make

a fire with driftwood. We can eat and drink and

have some well-earned fun.'

'An Operation Sweet Beach success party!'
Micky declared. 'Everyone, pose for a photo.
This is going in the Hall of Cute Cooperation
first thing tomorrow!'

Micky set the timer on the camera and the cutes all lined up.

'One, two, three, say CHEESECAKE!' Micky cried.

As the sun dipped, the cutes sat round their driftwood fire with cake on their knees and cups of cherry lemonade. They remembered the creatures they'd rescued during the day. The wibbly wobbly Sea Plops, the Tumbly Turtles, the Jelly Babies, the Spot Puffs . . .

'Don't forget me!' giggled the gherkin. 'You rescued me, too!'

'Imagine if you'd drifted out to sea and the sea monsters came . . .' Dee said ominously.

Lucky laughed. 'There's no such thing as monsters!'

'I know,' said Dee. 'But just imagine . . .'

As the sunset sizzled and the plum-coloured sky turned dark, most of the Operation Sweet

Beach crew returned to Charm Glade, leaving the small gang of super cutes to spend some precious time together. They wriggled their toes in the clean, silky sand and stacked more driftwood on the campfire. And Dee had a late-night surprise – ingredients for s'mores! They twirled their chocolatey marshmallow sticks over the embers and told stories. As the sky became freckled with stars, the stories got spookier and spookier.

'. . . and then, the shadow crept closer,' whispered Louis, getting to the end of his tale. 'I was frozen to the spot. I couldn't move an inch. My nose was like ice and my tail was stiff as a broom handle. And it came nearer and nearer, and suddenly –'

'WAAAA–OOOO–EEEE!'

'Wh-wh-what was that?' Lucky said.

The cutes leaped closer together as the wail came again – a hollow moan in the darkness.

Cami shuddered. 'Are you sure there's no such thing as monsters?' she said.

CHAPTER FOUR

The Tale of the Wail

'I'm scared,' moaned Cami. She rained miniature candles, which briefly lit up the faces of the cutes round the campfire.

Pip suddenly gasped. 'Sammy's missing!' she cried. 'What if he's been taken by a monster?'

The cutes screamed, which startled Sammy, who had fallen asleep and camouflaged himself against the sand. He leaped up, his coat flashing pink and purple in alarm, which made the cutes scream again.

'The monster!' shouted Louis.

Micky chuckled. 'It's just Sammy!'

'Well, something made that "waaaa-oooo-eeee!" sound,' said a quivering Cami.

'There's probably a perfectly good explanation,' said Sammy. 'Let's use logic. There's nothing scary in the World of Cute, is there? So therefore, whatever is making that noise cannot be scary.'

'If it's not scary, then perhaps it's . . . scared?' Pip suggested.

'That's a very good possibility,' Sammy said.

'I'm not sure,' Dee said. 'I've never heard a sound like that before. Perhaps it's something from outside the World of Cute. In which case, we should be very afraid.'

'There's no point in just guessing,' Pip said. 'Let's go and find out.'

'If we stick together, then we'll be safe no matter what,' Louis barked.

'Teamwork all the way,' Micky agreed.

'WAAAA—OOOO—EEEE!'

Holding hands, the super cutes tiptoed in the direction of the wailing. The wind had completely dropped, and the cry was crystal clear and easy to follow. It led them back up to the top of the beach and into the sand dunes.

They climbed to the
top of the largest dune and looked ·
down at the scrubby forest on the other side.
Most of the forest was lost in shadows. From
deep among the trees, the wailing continued.

'I can't see a thing!' Micky said, peering into
the gloom. 'We'll get covered in brambles, poked

in the eye by branches, tripped up by tree roots.'

'That's a bit dramatic, Micky!' Dee said.
Then she frowned. 'But I don't fancy getting
my wool tangled, my whiskers snared, my craft
pockets ripped!'

'Now who's being dramatic?' Pip said with a
giggle. 'Cami, can you see anything from up there?'

'No,' said the little cloud. 'But I can shed some light. Wait there.'

Cami melted up into the dark sky and returned moments later with a gaggle of baby stars. They spun above Cami's head like a halo.

'Do your thing, starlets!' said Cami.

The stars scattered above the dune sands, lighting a sloping path into the forest below. Pip jumped first, tumbling and rolling down. The others followed, one by one, until they were all at the bottom.

'WAAAA–OOOO–EEEE!'

The cutes felt scared again. They still didn't know what was waiting for them in the forest. They reached for each other's hands.

'WAAAA–OOOO–EEEE'

The cry was louder now.

Louis sniffed the air. His tail wagged furiously. 'That way, just over there!' he barked.

Cami whistled. The starlets clustered together to create a bright light that banished all the shadows. And as the star-glow spread in the trees, the cutes saw it.

There, standing all alone in a clearing, was a small seal. He had thick white whiskers and a speckled grey and black coat. A small felt hat sat at an angle on his head. His mouth was open, ready to wail again. When he saw the super cutes, he quickly shut it.

'H-hello?' he said nervously.

Sammy stepped forward, adjusting his spectacles. 'Sol, is that you?' he asked.

The seal just shivered, his wide round eyes glittering with panic.

'Who's Sol?' Dee whispered.

'He's one of the Intrepid Expedition Scouts,' said Sammy. 'Sol! It's me, Sammy.'

'Sammy, it might be a good idea if you

uncamouflaged yourself,' Lucky suggested.

'Oh yes.' Sammy shook the forest green from his fur and made himself a very visible yellow.

'Sammy!' Sol's face cracked into a wide grin. 'Am I glad to see you!'

'What are you doing out so late, Sol?' asked Louis with a friendly woof.

'Well, I was just earning my first solo expedition badge, crossing the Treacle Seas and circling the Remarkable Biscuit Islands, when a storm came out of nowhere,' said Sol. 'One minute I was happily sailing. The next, I was flying through the air. I didn't know if I'd landed on a Biscuit Island or somewhere completely off the map. But I'm here – in the World of Cute?'

'Yes, you are,' Lucky said sweetly. 'Welcome home, Sol.'

'Except this isn't home,' Sammy said. 'The Intrepid Expedition Scouts live on Good Rock Island, miles from these shores.'

'That's right.' Sol sniffed and his cheeks wobbled. 'The trouble is, if I'm not home by tomorrow evening, I'll miss the Starboard Ceremony. It's the end-of-expedition party where we get our badges and become Intrepid Expedition Scout Masters. If I miss it, I won't be allowed to go adventuring on uncharted seas with the rest of my friends. I'll have to redo the whole year!'

'Then let's get you home!' Pip said.

'We can use a map. I have lots of maps back at the museum,' Micky said.

'No, a map won't do. Um . . .' Sol looked around the clearing, at the bits and pieces that were left of his boat.

'If it's a boat you need, we can find you another one,' Dee said helpfully.

'It's not that,' Sol replied, his whiskers drooping. 'Only the Intrepid Compass can show me the way home. And I can't find it anywhere. My treasures are gone, too!'

Sol's eyes watered with worry. But he straightened himself with a great big sniff, and began to sing.

There once was a great intrepid seal

Who sailed the seas with lots of zeal

He washed ashore in the World of Cute

Without his Intrepid Compass true.

What shall become of him?

His future's looking kind of dim.

What shall become of him

Who lost his Intrepid Compass true!

Although it was a jolly shanty tune, the super cutes understood the pain behind the words. This ceremony meant everything to Sol! How did you help a seal get back to an island you'd never heard of?!

Pip felt it was time for leadership.

'We'll help you look for your compass,' she said. 'We can do anything when we put our minds to it.'

Louis began sniffing at the forest floor. 'What does it smell like?' he asked.

'I don't know!' Sol said, half-laughing and half-crying. 'But it's metal. Small, round and shiny.'

The starlets began to drift away.

'Come back!' Dee squealed. 'We need your light.'

'Their parents are calling them,' Cami sighed. 'They have to practise their star tricks while the sun is sleeping. We can't make them stay.'

As the last little star drifted away, the cutes were enveloped in gloom once more.

'I can't see anything clearly,' Micky said. 'I can barely see Sammy.'

'Sammy, are you camouflaged again?' Dee asked with a giggle.

'No, I'm luminous pink,' said Sammy. 'It's going to be impossible to hunt for anything in this darkness.'

'Can I make a suggestion?' Pip said. 'We're all tired from cleaning the beach all day, and Sol the seal has suffered a shock. Why don't we sleep now, and get up as soon as the sun rises? We'll have plenty of time and light to look for Sol's lost things. And we'll have more energy in the morning, too.'

'I agree!' said Micky.

'Me too,' said Lucky.

'Me three,' Louis said.

'Me four, and I'll make us some pretty tents in no time,' Dee said.

'I think it's a very sensible idea, Pip,' Sammy said. 'Sol?'

The seal sniffed loudly. 'I don't know. Everything is such a mess . . .'

Pip nudged him gently. 'Come on, Sol. Join us at our camp on the beach, and we promise we'll do everything we can to help you just as soon as dawn breaks.'

'Everything always looks brighter in the morning,' Micky added.

CHAPTER FIVE

Rise and Shine!

The sun rose, spreading its rays across the sandy ripples of the beach. It made Dee's colourful canvas huts glow like stained-glass windows. The boiled-sweet colours fell on the faces of the cutes as they all stretched from their slumber, blinking their eyes and yawning.

'Everyone up!' came a voice. 'Up, up, up!'

The cutes looked out of their tents. Sol was

running on the spot and doing knees-ups, looking remarkably graceful with his hat still in place.

'Rise and shine!' he called. 'Get those lungs full of air. Best way to start the day!'

'What are you waiting for, cutes?' cried Pip, joining Sol and launching into some star jumps. 'There's work to do!'

The cutes stumbled on the sand and copied Sol and Pip, stretching their bodies and limbering up. Then Lucky flew to the Shoo-Shoo Bakery Van and brought back a bag of pastries and fruits to fill them up.

'So where do we look for Sol's Intrepid Compass?' Dee purred through a flaky butter croissant.

'It must have flown out of the boat – either when I was in the air, or when the boat crashed into the forest,' Sol sighed.

'So whether it's in the sea, on the sand or down behind the dunes, it must be in the seaside area,' Sammy said.

Louis ran round in circles. 'My paws will upset the sand and turn up anything that might be underneath!' he panted.

'I'll have a swim and see if there's anything floating in the water,' said Pip. 'If Sol's Intrepid Compass did get lost at sea, it should have come in on the tide by now.'

'Cami and I will fly around and see if we

can see anything glinting in the sun,' Lucky suggested.

'Thank you all so much,' said Sol. 'I'll go back to the forest and check again there.'

'I like your organisation, Sol. And your hat,' said Micky. 'Sammy and I will come with you. If there's something to be found, we'll find it. Operation Sweet Beach won't finish its duties until everything is back in order. And that includes lost compasses.'

'Well said, Micky,' said Pip, doing a triple-flip. She landed perfectly. 'Wow, look at that! It's a good sign.'

The super cutes trawled the dunes, the forests and the sea foam, looking for Sol's special compass. Although they found many delightful things, like the cute Sand Bunnies that burrowed by the beach, and the edible morning dew-puffs of the dunes' sherbet flowers, they didn't see anything else. But they didn't give up.

The sun rose higher and higher. Sol marched up and down the beach like a sergeant major.

'Sol is being so brave, but he must be upset,'

Pip said to herself, watching Sol's whiskers twitch with worry. 'I need to say something to him. But what?'

She got out of the water and shook the droplets from her prickles. Then she cartwheeled across the beach towards the seal and landed on the sand with a . . . CRUNCH.

Sand didn't go CRUNCH, she thought. There was something hard underneath it.

"Over here!" Pip called to the others. "I've found something!"

Louis began scooping the spot furiously with his claws. In no time, the cutes had unearthed a very battered square suitcase covered with travel stickers. It looked as if it had been on wild adventures. Pip opened the case. Inside were binoculars and gold coins and trinkets and clothes.

'My treasures!' Sol exclaimed.

'Is the Intrepid Compass here, too?' Lucky asked in excitement.

'That's not where I kept it,' Sol said. 'BUT, if the treasure case landed here, there's a good chance it isn't too far away!'

Dee suddenly gasped. 'Look!' she said, pointing at a nearby rockpool.

It wasn't the Intrepid Compass. It wasn't the flippety-fish under the water, either. It was the reflection on top of the rockpool. Rainbow bubble hugs!

Everyone looked up. Bubble hugs were floating overhead.

As if flooded with warm, sweet fruit-tea, all of

the cutes sighed happily.

'The hug whales,' Cami said. 'The hug whales are here.'

The beautiful hug whales rarely came close to the shore. When they did, they were either being nosey, or they wanted to spread happiness in the form of their cuddly bubble hugs. This time it was both. All the beach action had distracted two hug whales on their annual migration, and they'd stopped to see what the fuss was about.

They were so pleased to see the cutes that they were streaming bubble hugs from their blow holes.

The bubble hugs rained down and popped on the cutes' heads. Everyone felt like they had been given a big, squishy hug.

'Hey, hug whales!' Lucky called. 'What brings you so close to the shore?'

'Just popping by to say hi,' the hug whales called, with voices that sang like soft whistles. 'And to see why you're all running up and down the beach like crabs on hot coals!'

'We're looking for something,' Pip said. 'A compass. Sol the seal lost it in the storm and he needs it to get home.'

'What does it look like?' said one of the hug whales.

'Small, round, shiny,' Sol said, his eyes widening with hope.

'We know someone who saw something small, round and shiny at the bottom of the sea,' said the largest of the hug whales. 'It could be what you're looking for . . .'

CHAPTER SIX

Follow the Hugs

The only thing standing in the way of the cutes and the Intrepid Compass was the big blue sea. But Micky knew Charm Glade's marine conservation expert, Ferg the green tree frog, who lent them his pretty submarine, the *Bella-Blue*.

The *Bella-Blue* was small and quick, with propellers on the front and back. The super cutes climbed into the capsule and Micky screwed the hatch shut. Everyone was packed tightly together and fidgety with excitement. They loved having new experiences together. And, as they looked out of the porthole windows into the bluest sea they'd ever seen, this promised to be the most thrilling yet! Dee miaowed with excitement and Louis barked, which rang in everyone's ears so he promised not to do it again.

'Who's steering?' Lucky asked.

'Pip has shown herself to be a wonderful leader. Perhaps she should take the controls,' Sammy said, smiling at the pineapple.

Pip would have flipped for joy if there had been room. 'I'd love to!' she said. 'If Sol will sit next to me. His navigating skills might come in useful.'

'I'd be delighted,' Sol said, nudging the edge of his felt hat with a flipper.

'Everyone ready?' Pip asked, settling herself in the control seat.

'Yay!' shouted the cutes. 'We're off to find the Intrepid Compass!'

'Ready when you are!' whistled the hug whales, swimming beside the submarine.

Pip chugged forward. Then she pushed the lever to angle the submarine downwards, following the hug whales into the depths of the Deep Cute Sea. There was a rush of bubbles as the top of the *Bella-Blue* sank beneath the waves . . . then everything was calm.

The cutes oohed and aahed as cube fish and squiddly-pigs drifted by the portholes. They passed myrtle turtles munching on clumps of sweet-and-sour seaweed. Every now and then, the hug whales blew their bubble hugs, which glittered and popped against the Bella-Blue's round glass windows, creating splurges of rainbow.

'How about some fun?' Pip asked.

'Wh-wh-what kind of fun?' Micky said nervously. He checked his seatbelt, because when Pip said fun, it usually meant something acrobatic.

He wasn't wrong.

'Hold on to your seats!' Pip called, pushing the levers hard.

The submarine nose-dived into a somersault. Pip pulled the levers sideways, so the *Bella-Blue* rolled into a spin. 'Relax!' she laughed,

seeing the other cutes' faces. 'It's perfectly safe, and now you know how it feels to be me!'

'Being you IS fun,' Cami giggled. 'Especially in water, where there's no hard landing!'

'Did you know the most acrobatic creature in the sea is the sponge dolphin?' said Sammy. 'It can swim to the bottom of the ocean, push its tail against the seabed, then torpedo through the water and so high into the air that it can do a hundred spins and still have time to knit a seaweed beanie.'

'Stop! Slow down!' called the hug whales.

'Shh, the hug whales are giving instructions,' Lucky said. 'Pip, you've just driven straight past them!'

'Don't worry,' said Pip. 'Everything is under control!'

She pulled the levers upwards and the submarine looped back into position behind the hug whales.

'Excellent skills,' Sol said, stroking his chin. 'You should think about joining the Intrepid Expedition Scouts!'

Blushing with pride, Pip carefully followed the hug whales, keeping the submarine slow and steady so as not to disturb the sea life. Spatula lobsters roamed the rocks beneath them. Sugar sharks with gummy chew teeth foraged in the brightly coloured candy corals.

The hug whales finally stopped and pointed at

the seabed with their tails. This was the place.

Pip turned off the engine and kept the *Bella-Blue* floating in position.

The water had changed from turquoise to dark blue. Below them, the sea floor dropped away.

Sol looked worried. 'This must be the Sapphire Trench,' he said. 'We learned about it at Intrepid Expedition School. It's too deep for submarines. The *Bella-Blue* can't take the

pressure of all that water.'

'Then what can we do?' Micky said.

'I think there's a solution,' Sammy

said, eyeing the hug whales outside. 'Hug whales, we need to swim down into the Sapphire Trench. Can you blow us some super bubbles?'

'What are super bubbles?' Cami asked.

'I guess we're about to find out,' Lucky said.

The first hug whale blew an enormous bubble that covered the whole of the *Bella-Blue*.

'Now, Lucky? Unscrew the hatch and step out into the bubble,' Sammy said. 'Trust me.'

Lucky looked nervous, but she knew that Sammy had all the facts and would never suggest anything this crazy if he wasn't sure it would work. She climbed out and stood on top of the *Bella-Blue*, inside the bubble. The bubble shrank and closed

around her, so she was floating in the sea in

her own rainbow capsule.

The super cutes cheered.

The second whale made another bubble,

ready to evacuate the next cute. One by

one, they left the *Bella-Blue* in their little

bubbles of safety, drifting on the underwater

currents. 'Steer it with happy thoughts!'

Sammy commanded.

The cutes happily steered their bubbles down, down, down into the Sapphire Trench. Strings of torch oysters lit the way like fairy lights. They passed strange deep-sea creatures that had adapted to the darkness

of the trench. Bright pink octopops hung in the water like plump, octopus-shaped jellies. Grumpy-faced spangle fish approached the bubbles with deep frowns and sharp teeth, making the cutes gasp. But spangle fish didn't often get to meet visitors so deep in the sea. Their menacing toothy grimaces turned into bright grins at the sight of the cutes, and the little lamps that hung above their heads flickered green and orange. Phosphorescent leopard eels with spotty patterns slithered between their bubbles. Swarms of flappy-eared dumbo slugs made luminous curtains with their long, trailing frills.

And then they were so deep, there was nothing but darkness.

'Lucky? Pip?' Cami called nervously. 'Where are you?'

'I'm over here,' Pip said, although she didn't know where over here was and she couldn't see anyone either.

'We need a light,' Micky said.

'Lucky, is there anything you can do?' Sammy asked. 'Without light to reflect colour, my fur is permanently camouflaged. I can't see myself, let alone anyone else.'

Lucky's horn could light up when the moon was out – but down here there was no moon. The only other time it worked was when she felt the power of friendship.

'Everyone?' said Lucky. 'We may not be able to see each other, but let's all say these words together. We're there for each other, in darkness and in light, in daytime and in night.'

The cutes' voices gathered together until they were chanting at the same time.

'We're there for each other, in darkness and in light, in daytime and in night.'

'Super cutes are the best of friends. Hooray!' added Dee.

As the chant got louder, Lucky felt their friendship tingle in her tail and wings. And in her nose. Her horn began to sizzle, and then . . .

FIZZ!

Her horn threw out sparks that stayed alight, filling Lucky's bubble. Soon it was so bright, it was like an underwater light bulb.

'You did it!' Pip squealed. 'Oh Lucky, how

lucky are we to have you as a friend!'

Lucky laughed. 'Don't overdo it. I might pop!'

Following Lucky and her bright bubble, the cutes reached the bottom of the Sapphire Trench, where a little glowing light throbbed beneath the sand.

'Could that be your compass?' Louis asked with excitement.

Sol frowned. 'I don't think so,' he said. 'It doesn't make light. It reflects light. But let's check it out just in case.'

Pip steered her bubble fast towards the trench floor. The moving water swooshed away the sand.

'You're right, Sol. It's not your compass,' Pip

sighed. 'It's a baby
star!'

'Poor thing!' said
Cami. 'It must have
been confused during the
storm. It probably thought the dark trench was
the midnight sky!'

The little star glowed sadly on the seabed.

'Let's get it home right away,' Micky said.
'Although I don't know how. We can't leave our
bubbles to collect it.'

'I've got an idea,' said Dee. She rummaged in
her pockets until she found a straw. 'Wish me
luck, everyone.'

'Good luck, Dee!' cried the other cutes.

With her paw over one end of the straw so water didn't rush in, Dee pushed the other end through her bubble until it was touching the star. Then she took her paw off her end. The star shot through the straw into the bubble. Dee quickly pulled the straw back in and her bubble closed over.

'Phew!' Dee said. 'It worked!'

Pip cheered. 'Brilliant, Dee! And I'm so glad the baby star is safe. But we still haven't found Sol's compass. And we can't rest until we do!'

CHAPTER SEVEN

Treasure Beyond Measure

When the super cutes were all safely back on board the *Bella-Blue*, they decided to go back to shore and continue to search for Sol's compass there. Time was running out. Sol had to get home in time for the Starboard Ceremony, to celebrate his achievement as an Intrepid

Expedition Scout Master!

Pip steered them back to land. She didn't do any tricks and flips this time. Everyone was worried about the time, and the baby star was still shaken up from being lost at the bottom of the sea for so long. Pip sat him on her lap and showed him all the submarine controls and told him about the creatures that passed by the porthole.

When they reached the shore, they waved goodbye to the hug whales. Then they all hugged the baby star before Cami led him back into the sky to his family.

'What do we do now?' Micky asked, looking nervously at Sol. The seal had gone a bit quiet.

'Let's go for a lemonade,' Dee said. 'I know it doesn't help get you home, Sol. But perhaps you just have to forget about the Starboard Ceremony now, and try to have a little fun.'

Sol coughed to cover up a sob. 'The Starboard Ceremony is everything to me,' he said.

'We understand,' Lucky said softly. 'But we've done all we can to get you there.'

'When you think you've done everything you can,' said Sammy, 'that's when you should give it one last go.'

'Is that a fact?' Louis asked.

Sammy chuckled. 'No. But it should be."

'It's worth a try,' said Pip. 'Operation Sweet Beach Two – who's in?'

'Me!' said Micky.

'Me too!' said Louis.

'All of us,' Sammy said hurriedly, to save time. 'All of us are in.'

'Then let's hunt!' Lucky said.

Full of hope and optimism, Sol the seal

bellowed beautiful sea shanties as they started the search again.

There once was a boat called the Bella-Blue

That steered its way so bold and true

It went to the bottom of the Sapphire Trench

To save a fallen star.

Hooray for cutes and friends

Who'll stay with you until the end

Hooray for cutes and friends

Who'll help the best they can.

'WHAT ARE YOU DOING?'

The super cutes looked up at the sound of that familiar snippy voice. Clive was standing at the edge of the beach, dressed in a whole new beach wardrobe, watching them with narrowed eyes. The Glamour Gang stood behind him, slurping strawberry slushies.

'I SAID,' Clive repeated, 'what are you DOING?'

The super cutes sighed. Ignoring Clive wasn't going to work this time.

The cheeky chihuahua tiptoed down the beach towards them in his high-heeled flip flops. His elaborate beach shawl flapped behind him like the wings of a great swan.

'I only just cleaned this beach,' he yapped. 'And now you're messing it up.'

Dee's fur shook with anger. 'YOU cleaned

this beach?' she said.

'Shhh, Dee,' Pip whispered. 'If this turns into an argument, we won't have time to find Sol's Intrepid Compass! In fact, Clive might be able to help us. He always turns things into a competition. We can make this work in our favour.'

The super cutes exchanged glances and nodded. It was the only way.

Lucky faced the little chihuahua. 'We've lost something on the beach, Clive,' she said.

'Well, it's a shame you don't have an incredible sense of smell like me, then,' said Clive. 'I can sniff out anything. I come from a long line of prize smellers.'

'A long line of prize stinkers,' Dee muttered under her whiskers.

'Well, I'm not sure a compass has a smell,' Micky said.

Clive stopped mid-slurp of his slushie. 'A what?'

'A compass.' Sol shuffled forward. 'It's round and silvery and very precious to me.'

The chihuahua made a strange gurgling noise.

'Clive, are you OK?' Lucky patted the pup on the back in case he was choking on his slushie.

Clive quickly smoothed his ruffled fur and patted down his shiny purple swimming costume. He struck a pose. 'Is there a trophy?' he said.

'A trophy?' Louis barked. 'What for?'

'For sniffing out the compass, of course,' said Clive. 'I'm willing to offer my services – but only if I win something.'

Pip wanted to triple flip and karate-chop the smoothie out of Clive's paws and all down his ridiculous costume. But then she saw Sol's whiskery face. It was hopeful and worried all at the same time. Time was ticking. The sun was going down.

'How long until the Starboard Ceremony, Sol?' Pip asked.

'An hour,' the seal mumbled.

Pip gulped. An hour to find the Intrepid Compass and get Sol back across the seas to

Good Rock Island? There wasn't a second to lose!

'Yes, Clive,' Pip said quickly. 'There'll be a prize for the first cute to uncover Sol's special compass.'

'Glamour Gang, assemble!' yipped Clive with excitement. 'Scooter, hold my slushie. Muffin, hold my beach gown.'

The Glamour Gang crowded round the chihuahua as he stripped off his accessories – beach bag, shawl, heeled flip-flops. When Clive was left in nothing but his hat, glasses and little swimming costume, he tiptoed on to the sand and stuck his nose in the air. He sniffed dramatically one way, then the next. He narrowed his eyes and flattened his ears like a detective chasing a lead. (Not a dog lead. A clue.)

'Is he . . . pretending to sniff?' Cami asked.

He's definitely up to something,' Sammy said.

Clive suddenly bounded off towards the upper end of the beach, where the sand met the path back to Charm Glade. He stopped at a spot, circled it three times and then started to dig.

'Wasn't that where we saw him digging yesterday?' Louis said.

The cutes ran up the beach to join the digging chihuahua.

'The compass is here. I know it is!' Clive panted, pawing at the sand.

'How do you know?' Louis challenged. 'I can't smell anything.'

'That's because you don't have a special nose like me,' Clive yipped, digging furiously.

'Or is it because you know something is buried there?' Pip asked.

Clive looked offended. 'Don't be silly,' he barked. 'I'm Clive, descendant of the Pawsdons and Barkalots and I am simply superior in my – hey, what are you doing?'

Louis had begun digging too. And Lucky. And Pip.

'Aha!' Sammy said. 'There it is.'

And there, at the bottom of the sandy pit, something flat, round and smooth shone in the afternoon sun. Sol's Intrepid Compass!

'You fetch it, Clive,' said Cami kindly.

Clive reached into the sandy hole and picked up the compass. He blew off the remaining sand with a little huffy puff and presented to Sol.

'I'm the winner,' Clive said.

We're all winners, thanks to you, Clive,' Sol said, his large eyes watering.

Clive blushed and gave a little cough. 'But I'm the number one winner, right?'

Lucky nudged Sol. Sol got the message.

'Yes Clive,' said Sol. 'You're the number one winner.'

CHAPTER EIGHT

Good Bye, Good Rock

Sol held up his Intrepid Compass. The super cutes watched as he calculated the directions, the weather and the time it would take to sail home. What an incredible compass it was!

This was the moment of truth. Would he get back in time for the Starboard Ceremony?

'Well?' Micky asked nervously. He hated it

when things didn't go according to plan.

'Well?' asked Lucky, flapping her wings impatiently.

'WELL?' they all cried.

'Well . . .' Sol said slowly, a grin stretching across his face. 'The weather is perfect and the stars are aligned. It looks as if I'll make it back with moments to spare!'

'That's brilliant!' Pip said, flipping so high with glee she lost control.

Sol caught her and placed her back on the sand. 'Now, one small but necessary detail . . .' he said. 'How will I find a boat?'

'I could try to make one,' Dee mewed.

'No need. The boat yard is just up there,'

Micky said, pointing up the beach. 'There are always spare boats for tours round the island.'

The super cutes ran to the boat yard and dragged a large wooden boat to the edge of the water.

'And now it really is time for me to go,' Sol said. 'But I don't want to leave you.'

'We are very special,' Clive agreed with a sniff.

'You have to attend that ceremony, Sol! It's everything you dreamed of,' Pip said. 'We have lots of memories. Go, before it's too late.'

'I mean, I want you to come with me,' said Sol, blushing. 'Come and see where I live. It'll be an adventure.'

'Who can resist an adventure!' Pip said. 'We'd

love to, wouldn't we, everyone?'

The super cutes looked at each other in surprise. A spontaneous adventure?

'New adventures, new experiences,' Pip urged. 'It's what we love. And wouldn't it be nice to be there at Sol's ceremony. It would be the greatest honour.'

'Yes,' gasped the others. 'YES YES YES!'

'Last on the boat's a smelly turtle poo!' said Louis. 'Hey, where is the boat?'

The evening tide had dislodged the boat from the sand and it was now drifting slowly out to sea!

'We'll have to swim for it!' Sol shouted happily. He slipped into the water and swam briskly to the boat. In no time he was standing on the boat deck, waving. 'Come on!'

'Ooh, a lovely swim!' said Sammy.

Clive's whiskers trembled. 'I think I'll sit this one out,' he said.

'Rubbish!' Pip declared. 'You have to come, Clive. After all, you found the Intrepid Compass.'

'And you're wearing the best swimming costume on the beach,' Dee said.

Clive started getting flustered. 'No, I, well . . . No. NOOOO!'

It was too late. Lucky and Cami had swooped in. Taking an arm each, they dragged Clive towards the waves. As the chihuahua screeched, everyone cheered and sang:

'For he's a jolly good cutie, for he's a jolly good cutie, for he's a jolly good cutie, and so say all of –'

SPLASH!

'My fur!' howled Clive. 'It's wet!'

'You can do it, Clive,' said Sammy encouragingly. 'Come on!'

Everyone began swimming towards the boat, where Sol was waiting for them with his hat

miraculously dry and still in place. Clive swam furiously but daintily, with his chin lifted as high as it could go. He looked like an angry meerkat. A wave washed right over his little head. When he popped back up again, he had lost his hat and glasses. He was barely recognisable.

Cami giggled. 'You look so funny, Clive!'

Clive's salty fur had fluffed up like a fuzzy halo. When he realised everyone

was laughing at him, he pulled out the pocket mirror he kept tucked into his bathers. He squealed in horror at his reflection.

'We weren't laughing at YOU, Clive,' Pip called. 'Just at the change in your hairstyle!'

Clive looked once again in the mirror. The cutes prepared themselves for one of his tantrums. Sure enough, his ears began to shake and his whiskers quivered. All that was left to come was the scream of annoyance. And that dog could scream! His angry little yips could freeze a hotdog and crack a toffee apple.

But there was no scream. Instead, Clive he began to chuckle. At first it was a little chuckle, but it grew louder and louder.

'Is that a weird kind of crying?' Louis asked. 'Shall we say sorry?'

'Clive, are you OK?' Lucky said.

The little dog began swimming again with his nose in the air.

'I'm more than OK,' he yipped, still chuckling. 'I'm FABULOUS! And you should look at yourselves!'

Sammy's blue camouflaged fur was waving around like seaweed. Louis looked more like an otter than a dog. Cami was so full of water, she was stretched tight like a balloon.

'You all look hilarious!' Sol called, slapping his paws together. 'But chop chop. The Intrepid Compass says we can't wait any longer.'

The cutes boarded the boat and shook the drops from their fur, ears, whiskers and snouts.

'And now, we set sail,' Sol announced.

'Wait! The boat needs a name,' Louis said. He leaned over the edge of the boat and used his paintbrush nose to write along the side: *Intrepid Friends Forever.*

'Lovely,' Sol said, raising the sails. He stood with one flipper on the giant wheel and the other holding his compass. 'Now hold on. I mean it. HOLD ON!'

The boat picked up speed. The wind whizzed by so fast, words were whipped from the super cutes' mouths. Their fur dried instantly. The colours of the sea and the sky melted into one.

Sol sang his shanties and turned his wheel and within minutes they were approaching a pool of glowing lights.

'Night Star Lagoon,' Sol shouted. 'The harbour of Good Rock Island. We're here!'

The sailing boat pulled into the harbour, which was a lagoon of a thousand colours. The colours swirled into each other and mixed to create more colours and the super cutes sighed with the beauty of it all.

'The water is like a magic potion,' Cami whispered.

'Good Rock Island is a magical place,' Sol said. 'That's why you can only find it using the Intrepid Compass. Without the Intrepid

Compass, there's no chance, because the island never stays in one place.'

'Oh Sol, I'm so glad Clive found your compass,' Lucky said. 'Imagine if he hadn't!'

'Imagine if he hadn't buried it in the first place,' said Dee. Pip gave her a look. Everything was going so well, it was best not to spoil it.

'Come on,' said Sol. 'Let me show you around before we head to the Starboard Ceremony.'

The harbourside was full of eating places. The cutes inhaled the delicious steam that rose from sharing plates spread out on the tables. There were farm greens with sticky savoury sauces, stews with rice, and dessert platters piled high with fruit and pastries.

'There are my friends,' Sol said, pointing to a group of seals sitting round one of the tables. 'Come and meet them.'

Sol introduced the cutes. His seal friends listened to the story of the storm and the beach hunt and the fallen baby star. They were so impressed at how the cutes had worked to get Sol home that they insisted on giving everyone beautiful gifts: necklaces made of sea glass and shells, stones in the shapes of hearts, edible seaweed baskets and conch shells that could be blown like horns.

'If you blow one of these three times, we'll hear you,' said a seal called Selly. 'And if we're not out on an expedition or an adventure, we'll always come and play.'

'That would be great,' Pip said. 'I hear you seals can do some great underwater tricks. I'd love to learn some.'

'Of course,' said another seal called Selina. 'And let me give you one more thing.' She placed a perfectly round oyster shell in the middle of the table. 'Who is your leader and why?'

Clive went to raise his paw. But when he saw all the others pointing to Pip, he lowered it.

'We don't have a leader,' Pip said with a blush. 'We're all equal.'

Sammy coughed for attention. 'This is true,' he said. 'However, today, you have shown us what to do and how to do it, Pip. You made us a team. You have been the best version of Pip the pineapple, and a totally perfect cute.'

'Then, Pip, you shall be in charge of this,' Selina said. 'Open it.'

Wiping a tear from her eye, Pip opened the shell. There in the middle, like a large silver pearl, sat a compass just like Sol's. It had a dial with compass points and magical symbols that glowed under Pip's touch.

'I'm the Head Scout,' Selina continued. 'And if you ever want to find Good Rock Island, then use this. You will always be welcome here. After hearing about your tireless efforts to help Sol and your brave travels to the bottom of the Sapphire Trench, I have decided that you are

ALL now honorary Intrepid Expedition Scouts.'

The super cutes looked at each other with open mouths. They could find this magical place any time they liked? WOW!

Sol smiled warmly at them. 'I'm proud to call you my friends,' he said. 'Now, it's time for the Starboard Ceremony!'

The Starboard Ceremony took place at the Great Hall. The cutes took their seats in the crowd as the ceremony began with music from a water quartet, which filled the hall with the beautiful sound of harps, flutes and glockenspiels. And then came the presentation.

Selina, dressed in a long gown embroidered

with symbols that made Clive gasp with envy, stood at a podium. She called up the Intrepid Expedition Scouts, one by one. When it was Sol's turn, the super cutes all cheered loudly.

'Welcome Sol,' Selina said. 'You have travelled far and returned safe. You have earned your badge, and move up a level in your learning. You are now an Intrepid Expedition Scout Master.'

Selina saluted, raising her flipper to one brow and stroking it down her nose. Sol took the badge and returned the salute, raising his flipper to his brow and sliding it down his nose, before placing it against Selina's flipper for a high five.

The audience clapped and the cutes danced up and down with joy. Outside there was the bang and fizz of fireworks. The Starboard

Ceremony display had begun.

Sol leaped off the stage to greet his friends.

'Let's go watch the fireworks breaking over the lagoon!' he cried. 'You've never seen anything like it!'

Incredible fireworks ballooned and boomed over the magical swirling lagoon. When the

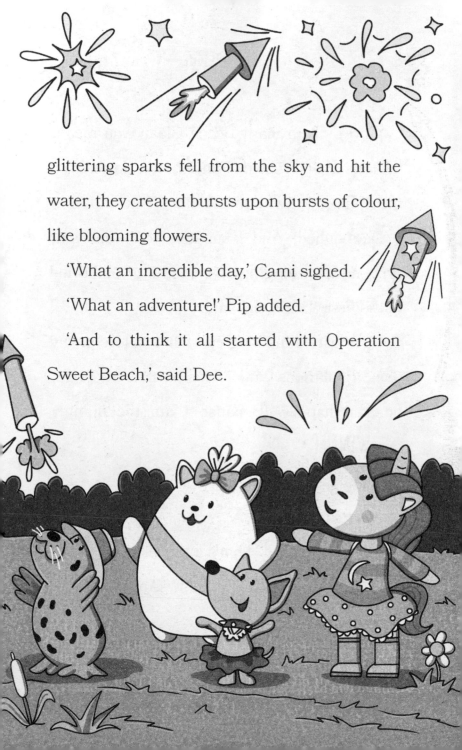

glittering sparks fell from the sky and hit the water, they created bursts upon bursts of colour, like blooming flowers.

'What an incredible day,' Cami sighed.

'What an adventure!' Pip added.

'And to think it all started with Operation Sweet Beach,' said Dee.

'Clive's Glam-Slam Beach Clean, you mean,' the little dog prompted. 'Funny how it started with me AND ended with me, finding that compass.'

Dee sighed. 'And I suppose you want your prize now, for digging up something you buried in the first place?' she said.

Clive batted his long eyelashes before giving one big hilarious wink. 'This party is my prize,' he said happily. 'Because I am the number one WINNER.'

'This day gets my seal of approval,' said Pip with a grin.

Micky chuckled. 'That's a terrible joke.'

'Cute though,' said Lucky. 'And that's all that's important!'

After long, huggy goodbyes with Sol and his friends and promises to meet up again, the cutes returned to the *Intrepid Friends Forever*. The warm breeze whistled sweetly in the sails. High above the mast, a little baby star winked and giggled.

Pip pulled her own Intrepid Compass from her pocket and held it up.

'It's been a whirlwind of a day,' she said softly. 'But now it's time to go home.'

And the friends set sail towards the wonderful World of Cute.

Read an exclusive extract of The Kindness Carousel!

CHAPTER ONE

Just in the Middle of a Dream

Inside a little house that swung from a branch of the liquorice tree, Cami the cloud was dreaming a glorious dream . . . She was having a picnic in the dipsy daisy meadows as the popsicle parrots circled above, filling the sky with rainbow colours. Her very best friends were there, which made it the best kind of dream, and she was about to take a bite of a dreamy sugar puff peach, when – TINKLE TINKLE TINKLE – a noise woke her up.

Cami was absolutely certain that the delicate chime was the sound of sweetie pies as they put-putted across the morning sky. And what was that rustling and bustling? It must be the World of Cute waking up!

Cami stretched out her cloud fluff. Then it dawned on her. She sprang out of her snooze basket and bumped her fluffy head on the ceiling.

'Oh my goodness, today is the fair!' she cried. 'THE SUNFLOWER FAIR!'

She flew quickly out of her house.

But instead of daylight, she found herself floating in the deep, dark blue sky that belonged to night. The tinkling she had heard was not the giggle of early morning sweetie pies, but the sound of the stars playing twinkle-chase. The rustle and bustle was not the World of Cute waking up, but the snuffles of allsort bugs, fast asleep in the nooks of the liquorice tree.

'Oh! I'm awake far too early,' Cami said sadly.

She floated back into her little home, sank into her soft basket and tried to get back to sleep. But it was impossible. Every time she closed her eyes, her imagination danced with colours and sounds and oodles of excitement. The Sunflower Fair was just hours away!

Cami had never been to the Sunflower Fair before, but her friend Sammy the sloth had told her all about it. It celebrated the start of summer, and it was all about happiness and sunshine. There were fairground rides and games, fun competitions and treats of every flavour imaginable. Everyone wore something that made them feel summery.

Best of all, Cami loved the sound of the glow cakes. They were made only once a year by the Sunshine Cakery: a secret bakery hidden deep in the buttercup fields, run by talented sugar mice and honey combs.

Cami smiled woozily as she remembered Sammy's description of the delicacy. *'The icing is so bright it makes you leap for joy; the topping is so fizzy it makes your tongue tingle; the middle is so yummy it makes your tummy gurgle . . .'*

Cami imagined leaping, giggling and gurgling with her friends as they munched the delicious treats under the new summer sun.

'I'm going to be the only cloud in the sky!' Cami said to herself in delight. 'But I'll be white and puffy and filled with nothing but happiness. It's going to be the most perfect day ever. And best of all, I'm sharing it with the super cutes!'

She snuggled down in her cloud basket, closed her eyes and thought back to the time she'd first met her special friends on the way to the Cuteness Competition in Charm Glade. Although everyone had started off nervous and shy, by the end of the day they were jumping with joy and happy to have made some new friends. It was the start of something truly special. Their next get-together had been Sammy's magical, mystical sleepover party, and then came the Friendship Festival, and the Adventure Weekend at Cute Camp . . . Whenever the super cutes were together, they always managed to have the best time.

By the time Cami had finished thinking all these happy thoughts, her brain was buzzing so much that there was absolutely no chance of going back to sleep.

'It's no good,' she said to herself. 'I'm just too excited!'

'Shhh,' hissed Albi, an allsort bug whose snooze hole was just outside her door. 'We're trying to sleep.'

'Sorry, Albi!' said Cami, her cloud fluff blushing. 'I'm so sorry.'

'If you stop saying sorry, I might be able to get back to sleep.'

She popped her head out of the door of her little house and looked up. Yes, there were the flocks of sweetie pies, lemony-yellow custard tartlets with meringue wings. They left icing sugar trails as they spun on the air currents. Above them, a big blue sky stretched from Vanilla Valley to Marshmallow Canyon to the Sandy Beaches and beyond.

'Perfect. Absolutely perfect!' Cami squealed.

She flew out and up into the air. The sun warmed the dew on her cloud fluff, making her steam like a dumpling and sparkle like a gummy glitter chew.

'Yippeeeee!' she cried, loop-the-looping over and over again. 'It's here! It's here!'

'What's here?' grumbled Albi the allsort bug, emerging from his dark hole to see what the fuss was about.

'The Sunflower Fair!'

To be continued in
The Kindness Carousel . . .

Check out more ADVENTURES with the Super Cutes!

CAUSING CHAOS IN A WORLD OF CUTE!

SUPER CUTE
FUN IN THE SUN

PIP BIRD

CAUSING CHAOS IN A WORLD OF CUTE!

SUPER CUTE
THE ADVENTURE SCHOOL

PIP BIRD

CAUSING CHAOS IN A WORLD OF CUTE!

SUPER CUTE
THE KINDNESS CAROUSEL

PIP BIRD

CAUSING CHAOS IN A WORLD OF CUTE!

SUPER CUTE
THE SEASIDE RESCUE

PIP BIRD

Enjoyed Super Cute? Check out these other brilliant books by Pip Bird!

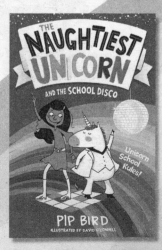

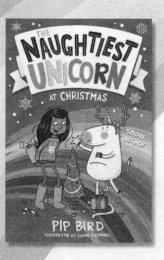

COMING SOON!

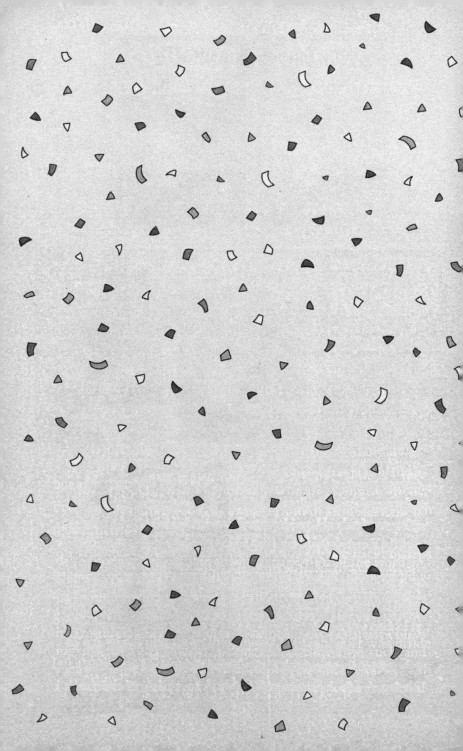